Many Happy Returns

Eighteen-year-old Lewis Oluwale Babatunde, also known as Tunde (*tune-day*), has just entered the second semester of his senior year of high school. With graduation quickly approaching and a resume that includes being Senior Class Vice President and Co-Captain of the basketball team, the possibilities are endless...right? Except things aren't exactly going as planned, leaving Tunde unsure of what his next step should be.

Until along comes a senior project that just might hold the answer to what lies ahead for him.

Text copyright 2022 by David Dada

Cover art illustrated by Randi Wilson

Visit the author's website at daviddadabhm.com

All rights reserved. Published in the United States.

ISBN 9798218049850

For my Aunt Bonnye "Ruth" Stitt.

"The universal Yoruba belief was that the adults of a lineage held all its things in trust for its living and yet unborn children…respectful references were commonly made to 'the ones who went before' and 'the ones who will come,' and some of the latter were regarded as direct reincarnations of some of the former—a belief often expressed in the names given to new babies."
—*A History of the Yoruba People*

Chapter 1

Happy Eighteenth Birthday to you, Lewis. Have a great day, and Many Happy Returns.

Dad always puts *Many Happy Returns* on my birthday cards. I didn't know what it meant until I Googled it and found that it "offers the hope that a happy day being marked would recur many more times." Dad also says it's something people say regularly back in Nigeria. Hopefully today will be a good day, and I need this to be a good year. I'm not heavy into New Year's resolutions, but with my birthday being in January, it's a good time to see where I am on my goals, especially this year.

But before I get into that, let me introduce myself. My name is Lewis Oluwale Babatunde. It's pronounced *loo-wis oh-loo-wha-lay ba-ba tune-day*. But almost everyone calls me Tunde. Every now and then I get a Tundy, but it's really pronounced *tune-day*.

Lewis was my mom's dad's name. I never got to meet him because he died before I was born, but everyone tells me he's where I get my height from. He was six-seven, and I've been six-five since ninth grade. I'm hoping this is the year where I get those extra two inches though because that would help with reaching my number one goal, but more on that later.

Granddad Lewis…I just realized that's the first time I've ever called him Granddad. It's not intentional. I never got to meet either of my granddads, so it's not a word I've had a lot of practice saying. Anyway, he was apparently handsome and known for being well-dressed. Growing up, anytime I would go to church with my great-aunts—his sisters—they would always say I looked "sharp just like Junior," his nickname, and that always felt kind of cool.

Oluwale is my dad's name too. It means "My God has come home" in Yoruba, which is our tribe in Nigeria. Dad came to the U.S. from Nigeria for college and met my mom here in Birmingham, Alabama. Eventually, they got married and had me and my little sister Ìfẹ́. Her name is pronounced *ee-fay*. I've never asked for more details on how my parents met, but Ìfẹ́, who is three years younger than me and already in love with the idea of love, asked as soon as she was old enough to understand what dating was. She always says I'll eventually want to know the story, and though I'd never admit it to her, she's probably right. But that time isn't now, and I'm good with that.

Babatunde is a traditional Yoruba name. *Baba* means father, and *Tunde* means returns, so when the name is given to a baby, it means that the spirit of the grandfather or another male ancestor has returned in the child.

So now that we've finished the mandatory Ancestry.com report I have to give whenever I introduce myself, I can get to some other facts about me. I'm from Birmingham, Alabama. I'm a senior at Ramsay High School, and ball—basketball to be specific—is life.

Well, let me clarify because at first glance, that makes it sound like I have NBA dreams, and I don't. I honestly don't think I've ever seriously dreamt of going to the league beyond fourth grade on career day when I said I wanted to be an NBA player and a missionary.

My folks have always talked about being more than an athlete, and I'm with that. I'm on the debate team. I'm senior class vice president, and I volunteer as a reading coach for younger kids at the library in our neighborhood. I know my career will eventually be something other than playing basketball, even though I'm not exactly sure what yet.

What I do know is that I love hooping, and my number one goal is to get a basketball scholarship to college. After college, I'll be fine with hanging it up. So, I guess it would be more accurate to say ball is adolescence, but clearly that doesn't have as good of a ring to it.

I went to a skills camp last summer, and I haven't been able to get what one of the coaches said out of my head: "Listen up, there's a million guys six-three and under who can play, about half a million who are six-five, and about half that who are six-seven. Once you get to six-nine, that's where it starts becoming rarer, but there are still a lot of elite-level guys."

His point was that all these guys are fighting for the same number of scholarships each year, so I'm thinking that those two additional inches from Granddad Lewis would strengthen my chances. I wouldn't turn down four to six inches to get into that six-nine to six-eleven range, but I'm not exactly holding my breath for that to happen. However, I do make sure to avoid anything that may stunt my growth, like coffee. Ifẹ́ is always going on and on about her lattes and macchiatos, but I don't mess with the stuff.

My first-ever recruitment letter for basketball came last year from The University of Chicago. It felt great to open it up and see my name, but they're Division III and don't offer athletic scholarships. They reached out because they were impressed by my ACT scores and grades, which is cool, but I'm still holding out for a basketball offer. I'm getting a little worried the closer I get to graduation though.

Mom doesn't share my worry at all. She's told me and Ìfẹ́ for as long as I can remember that we'll get academic scholarships. Even before we knew what that meant, she would just say it whenever any conversation about college came up. Eventually, I just started to believe it, so once the academic letters started coming, it didn't feel like a surprise. Mom doesn't mind my hoop dreams though. She's actually the one who got me into watching basketball. As long as I keep my grades good, she's good. It's like she's told every coach since I started

playing: "We're not raising a basketball player. We're

raising a young man who happens to play basketball."

I just found out about a high school coach in

Arkansas who reached out to her and Dad when I was

twelve guaranteeing I'd get a Division I scholarship if

they sent me to play for him. Of course, she said no, and

the only reason I even know about it is because Dad

saw something about Arkansas on TV the other day that

made him remember. I wasn't even mad because I

wouldn't have wanted to do that anyway, but when I

asked why she didn't tell me, she said, "I didn't need

your permission to tell him no."

That's Mom in a nutshell. It's always love, but

don't ever get confused about who's in charge.

I think that's the Birmingham in her—North

Birmingham to be exact, Collegeville to be even more

specific. Mom is the second oldest of six—three brothers

and three sisters. She never goes into much detail about

what it was like growing up other than saying there were times where they had to just do what they could to get by.

After graduating from high school, she paid her way through junior college and nursing school and worked at Carraway Hospital until it closed. Carraway was in North Birmingham, too, in a neighborhood called Norwood that's about five minutes from Collegeville. My grandma bought a house in Norwood right up the street from Carraway when Mom was sixteen that Mom lived in until she finished nursing school. Grandma lived in that same house until she died last year.

I always felt like part of the reason Mom chose to work at Carraway was to be able to take care of people from the north side like her. She's a great nurse too. Last year I found a folder she keeps in her room full of thank you notes from Carraway patients. There were at least fifty, but I lost count after that because I got so caught up in reading all the nice things they were saying about her.

Mom says I'll eventually find something I love as much as she loves nursing, but I'm still looking for now.

Even though the hospital's closed and the building has been vacant for years, Carraway still has the huge blue star on the top of the main building that you can see from pretty much anywhere in the city. Mom told me that the star used to be one of the first signs that let pilots know they'd made it to Birmingham.

After Carraway closed, Mom started working at UAB Hospital over on the southside of the city. I still think of her and Grandma whenever I see the star though.

I haven't been on the north side as much since Grandma died, but there's a lot of change happening. I heard on the news recently that somebody bought the Carraway building and is planning to turn it into a mixed-use development with condos, shops, and entertainment venues. I was just glad to hear that they're going to keep the star. I remember learning in school that what makes the North Star so special is that while everything around

it is constantly moving, it stays almost completely still.

That's why before maps and GPS were available,

travelers could always depend on the North Star to make

sure they were headed in the right direction. I guess

that's kind of what the Carraway star is like for me, so it's

good to know that even with everything else changing in

my life, I can still count on the star to be there.

Chapter 2

The only thing I may love more than basketball is reading. I've been hooked ever since the weekly trips I took as a kid to the Pratt City Branch of the Birmingham Public Library. Ìfẹ́ and I would check out as many books as we could fit in both hands and come back the next week to do it all over again. It would be impossible for me to pick a favorite book of all time, but my favorite right now is one I got from my aunt Ruth about the Fab Five, the early nineties University of Michigan basketball squad that started five freshmen.

Aunt Ruth loves basketball and reading just like me, so we've always been tight. I've been a University of Michigan fan ever since I found out she went there, and it's also a perfect fit because I already wear a lot of yellow and blue anyway. Aunt Ruth bought me a navy-blue Michigan hat with the yellow M on the front last year that I've worn at least a couple times a week since then.

That can get me some sideways looks living in Alabama, but it is what it is.

Aunt Ruth and I also vibe because she's like the family historian. My mom's dad—sorry, I mean Granddad Lewis—was Aunt Ruth's uncle, so she's technically my cousin. But since Aunt Ruth is basically the same age as Mom, Ìfẹ́ and I call her our aunt. Whenever our family in Birmingham travels to visit our relatives in the country, Aunt Ruth always fills us in about the people we're going to see, along with stories about going to see them when she was growing up.

I know hearing me say "in the country" may make some people roll their eyes and say "Isn't all of Alabama country?" First, no it's not. There are levels, trust me. Second, I mean no disrespect to the country or my people there. Those visits are some of my favorite times. I just use the term *country* because that's how everyone in my family describes it.

But anyway, Aunt Ruth is awesome. I actually spoke with her the other day while I was working on the senior project for my Capstone course. Capstone is a big deal at Ramsay. It's different from every other course because it's not based on a specific topic like math or science. Instead, it's supposed to bring together everything we've learned since freshman year. There's a different teacher selected for it every year, and each senior class always has a different project. At the end of the year, there's a big Capstone Day program where the rest of the school comes together to see the seniors present.

This year's teacher is Mr. Dunbar, who is hands down one of the coolest teachers I've ever had. He's a black guy, around six-three, and probably in his mid-forties. He's retired from the Navy, but his demeanor is more coach than drill sergeant. He is known for putting students on the spot to see if they're prepared, but as long as you are, his class is a good time.

Mr. Dunbar loves to travel, and his classroom is full of family pictures from different vacations they've taken. He has a wife and three daughters, and I say this in the most respectful way possible, his wife is *soooo* fine. Whatever word you have for *beautiful*, Mrs. Dunbar is that and more. I know I just went on a tangent, but she's worth it, believe me.

If you ever want to get him going, all you have to do is mention Chicago. He's from the Southside—Seventy-ninth and Chatham to be specific—and he's happy to let you know about it. It's actually cool to hear him talk about it though—except for the food.

Don't get him started on the food. He's always talking about some spot called Harold's Chicken Shack and their mild sauce that would apparently "put anywhere in Birmingham to shame." I find that hard to believe given how well acquainted I am with wing spots. I live on the westside of Birmingham, which is like the wing capital. Seriously, I'm willing to bet we have more wing spots per capita than any other place in the world.

Either way, questionable taste in wings aside, Mr.

Dunbar is a solid guy.

This year's project is to conduct oral history

interviews with two elderly women and prepare a

presentation based on what we learn. Mr. Dunbar said

the reason for the assignment is that the histories of

women, especially women of color, are often ignored

altogether or skimmed over without paying any real

attention to detail. We just got the assignment last week,

and judging from our class discussion, it seems like most

of my classmates are picking either one or both of their

grandmas as their choices.

I would do the same thing if I could, but Grandma

Jean, Mom's mom, died last year. I never even got to

meet Dad's mom, Grandma Ìfẹ́, because she died back

in Nigeria when I was two. Between church, school, and

our neighborhood, there are a lot of women I could

choose from though, and I've been trying to think

through options since last week. But for some reason my mind keeps coming back to my grandmas.

Maybe it's a sign. There's technically nowhere in the assignment that says the people we select *must* be alive, although that probably could be assumed. I've learned a lot about people who aren't alive anymore though. That's what we've done in basically every history class I've ever taken, so I guess it's not too crazy of an idea. The toughest part would just be the actual interviewing. Mom and Dad are always talking about how weighing pros and cons can help me make better decisions. I'll give it a shot.

Pros

❖ I'm already interested in learning more about Grandma Ìfẹ́ and Grandma Jean.

❖ Mom and Dad can help me fill in the gaps for any questions I have.

❖ I could get started right away since I technically
don't have to set up an interview time.

Cons

❖ Both of my "interviewees" have passed away.

Well, the pros outweigh the cons. The more I
think about it, the more excited I am about the
possibilities. I was getting ready to write some ideas
down for how I could get started the other night after
basketball practice when my phone rang, and I saw it
was Aunt Ruth.

"Hey Aunt Ruth. How are you doing?"

"I'm doing well. Just getting done with dinner. I
was talking to your mom the other day, and she
mentioned that you all have a big game coming up."

"Yes, ma'am. The playoffs start next week. Are
you going to be able to make it?"

"I wouldn't miss it for the world. I still remember going to your first pee-wee league game, and now you're a senior in high school. Who are y'all playing?"

"We're playing Parker."

"Now why did they have to go and match y'all up against the Thundering Herd? You know that's my alma mater, don't you?"

Of course, I know that Parker is Aunt Ruth's alma mater, and she knows that I know. In case I ever forget, all it would take is stepping one foot inside the shrine to Parker High, also known as her house, to remind me.

Arthur Harold Parker High School, also known as A.H. Parker High School or just Parker, was the first public high school for black people in the city of Birmingham. Their colors are purple and white, and their mascot is the Thundering Herd. The school is named after its first principal, Dr. Arthur Harold Parker, a black man whose statue sits right outside the front of the school. There are so many pictures of Dr. Parker in Aunt

Ruth's house that I grew up thinking he was a member of our family. She also has a framed article about Parker High in her living room from a 1950 edition of *Ebony* magazine and the headline is "The World's Largest Negro High School" because at that time, Parker had over three thousand students enrolled.

Growing up in Birmingham, I learned from conversations I overheard adults having that most of the white families that used to live in the city and send their kids to city schools had moved out to the suburbs and started their own school systems. Mr. Dunbar's class was the first time I actually had someone put the numbers in front of me though. Our class learned that between 1960 and 1970, Birmingham's population dropped for the first time in the city's history, going from around three hundred and forty thousand citizens to about three hundred thousand even. More than seventy-five percent of that drop was from white people leaving the city, and by 1980, the majority of the city's population was black.

Of course, all of this happened way before I was born, so the only Birmingham I've known has been one with city schools that are led by black principals and attended by mostly black students. It hasn't always been like that though, but the one constant has been Parker High School. It was founded in 1900, and until the 1930s, it was the only public high school option available to black people in the city.

Almost everybody I know from Birmingham has at least one family member who graduated from Parker. Aunt Ruth isn't the only one for me. Grandma Jean, Grandad Lewis, and almost all of my great-aunts and great-uncles went there too. I've even got teammates whose parents went to Parker. The school is just such a part of the culture in the city that even with them being our rival, there's respect.

My introduction to the rivalry happened during my freshman year at Ramsay's first road game against Parker. The game was packed, and it was easily the loudest environment I had ever played in up to that point. I was getting up to head to the free-throw line after a hard foul that had taken me to the ground. It wasn't a dirty play or anything, just the result of two guys colliding at full speed. As I was getting up, I heard a woman's voice yelling at the referee saying, "that wasn't a foul" and how I needed to "man up." That was nothing worse than I'd heard playing basketball at the park, so I just tried to block it out and focus on making my free throws.

After making both, I turned in the direction where the voice was coming from, thinking I would get a quick wink in at whoever the heckler was.

But when I laid eyes on the lady, I literally froze in place for a few seconds out of shock and respect for my elders. She had to be at least sixty years old, and she was in purple and white from head to toe. My first thought was that it couldn't possibly be her—until she winked at me and joined in chanting with the Parker cheerleaders like she was a senior in high school all over again.

That's Parker though. You've gotta love it. So, I couldn't help but smile as I replied to Aunt Ruth's clearly disingenuous question. "Yes, I know that's your alma mater."

"Alright. I was just making sure," she said with a petty laugh. "You know I'll be there to support you. I'll just keep my coat on over my Parker sweatshirt."

Aunt Ruth and I both laughed and then said our goodbyes, and it wasn't until I had put the phone down that I thought about how I should have asked for some advice on my Capstone Day project. As much as Aunt Ruth loves history, she would probably have some great ideas on how I can get started.

I'll make sure to follow up with her after our playoff game. Right now, I've got to go outside and practice my free throws. The game is at Parker, and I

need to be ready in case I run into my old friend from the

stands again.

Chapter 3

Thundering Herd Outlast Rams 81–76

in OT Thriller Between City Rivals

The Parker Thundering Herd advanced to the Class 5A subregional with a close win over the Ramsay Rams last night. The matchup was the third this season between the two teams, with them having split the previous two games. The game lived up to its billing as a face-off between two well-coached, senior-laden teams and was a back-and-forth duel with there being fifteen lead changes from the opening tip-off to the final buzzer.

The momentum appeared to swing in favor of the Rams after the game was sent into overtime by Ramsay senior Lewis Babatunde making two free throws to tie the game at 70 after being fouled as time expired. However, the Thundering Herd used their trademark hounding defense to hold Ramsay to only six points in the final period while extending their lead for good. Parker was led by junior Greg Harris' 22 points and eight assists, while Ramsay was led by Babatunde's 18 points and 10 rebounds. Ramsay finishes the season with a record of 21 wins and 11 losses, while Parker, 25–7, advances to play the winner of tonight's game between John Carroll and Wenonah.

I still can't believe it's all over…just like that. I woke up hoping it was all just a bad dream, but it's not. To say I've been in my feelings would be an understatement, but thankfully talking to my friend Juice always lightens my mood, even if it's because he usually has something crazy to say that makes me forget what I was thinking about.

His real name is Trent, but I've always known him as Juice. The name comes from when a football coach told him that he ran just like the "Juice," O.J. Simpson. When Juice told me the story of how he got his nickname, I didn't even know who O.J. Simpson was. I could definitely see the similarities once I went and looked up O.J.'s football highlights on YouTube though.

We've been cool since the first day of fifth grade when we first started going to the same school. He'd already been there, but I was new, and I remember not knowing anybody on the first day until I saw Juice. I'd never spoken to him, but I remembered his face from playing basketball against him in one of the local youth leagues. He walked over to me, introduced me to his friends, and eventually, they became my friends too.

I've always appreciated how he looked out that day. Being ten years old and the new kid is hard enough but adding in having a last name like Babatunde can make it an absolute nightmare. Juice never joked on my name though, although some of my other classmates were happy to fill the void left by his kindness with slander of their own. Either way, we've been tight ever since.

Juice is getting recruited heavily for football, and it makes sense because the little kid that the football coach noticed has grown into a six-two running back with the same stride. He's trying to decide where to go, but I've noticed he hasn't talked about it much around me over the last few weeks. I think it's because he doesn't want me to feel bad about not having any offers for basketball yet. I appreciate him looking out, but I'm honestly really happy for him. That's my guy.

"Tunde, have you thought any more about that camp I mentioned to you?"

"The football camp? Juice, I appreciate you looking out, but I told you, I'm a hooper, not a football player."

"You're a hooper now, but you're also six-five and two hundred and twenty pounds. If you give me a few months, I could turn you into a wide receiver, and I guarantee you'd get some Division I offers."

"Bro, I don't even know if my hands are good enough to be a wide receiver."

"You're six-five. You don't need to be OBJ. You'll mostly be catching jump balls, and if you can't catch, I'll teach you to hit, and you can be a defensive end."

"Learning to hit at eighteen doesn't seem like the best idea, especially if the guys I'd be up against have been playing their whole lives."

"You're overthinking it. Once you get out on the field, your instincts will take over. It's like Coach says, 'It's all about establishing dominance.' If you're in a hit-or-be-hit situation, you'll learn."

"Again, bro, I really appreciate you, but I'll pass."

"Okay. I'm just saying, there will be a lot of college coaches at the camp looking for prospects, so if you change your mind, just know I got you."

Juice isn't the first person to try to get me to play football, just the most persistent. He's been trying to convince me since middle school, but I've always told him and everyone else that my folks made me choose one sport so that I could focus on school.

That was true in sixth grade, but once I showed I could play sports and still make A's, I'm pretty sure I could've convinced them to let me give football a shot. The thing is, I really wasn't interested at that point. Watching football is cool, and of course in Alabama, it's everywhere, but I've never had the desire to play. Either way, Juice checks in regularly to see if I've changed my mind.

"By the way, if you're such a hooper, why do you love wearing that Detroit Lions jersey so much?"

"Because their cornerback Jeff Okudah is from the crib."

"The crib, as in Nigeria? Isn't he from Texas?"

"You know what I mean, bro. He's got Nigerian roots."

"But why the Lions though? If you're going to pick a team, you could at least pick a winner."

"I'm not a Lions fan. I'm a fan of Jeff Okudah, and since he plays for them, I root for them. If he went to another team, I'd probably buy that jersey too."

"Okay. What about that Jalen Ramsey LA Rams jersey? Is he Nigerian too?"

"Not that I know of, but he could be. I bought that jersey because the Rams colors are blue and yellow. You know the vibes."

"True. Alright. I'll let it go. Just know I got you if you change your mind about the camp."

"I appreciate it, bro. I'll let you know."

I don't know how to explain it, but I really do feel a connection to other Nigerians—and just other Africans in general. I feel like we understand some things about each other, just off the strength of our similar upbringing. So even if I don't know them personally, there's certain things I can just assume they're familiar with, like having your name mispronounced annually on the first day of class.

It's not too different from the way that I can relate to other American black people whether I know them or not based on similar experiences. Either way, there's just something in me that loves to see them do well.

Talking to Juice definitely took my mind off things though, if only for just a moment. Issa no for me as far as the football camp, but his intentions are good, and I appreciate that.

It turned out that Juice wasn't the only one who wanted to discuss my plans for the future today though. Mr. Dunbar told me during class that he wanted me to meet with him during fourth period to discuss my Capstone project. He's already given me the okay to move forward with choosing my grandmas after having me write out a plan for how I think I can make it work. During the season, fourth period is usually reserved for basketball practice, but now that it's over, I actually don't mind having something to take my mind off everything for a while. Plus, prom is coming up, and I don't have a date yet, so I may ask him if Mrs. Dunbar has any nieces who may be in town from Chicago next month.

Just kidding, but really though.

The first thing Mr. Dunbar mentioned after asking me how I was doing was the game. He said he was proud of the way we represented ourselves and the school. I thanked him, but I didn't say anything else about it because I was hoping he would change the subject. The next part of the conversation is what really threw me for a loop though.

"Lewis, after reading your project plan, I must say you are a very gifted writer who seems to have a real interest in research."

"Thanks, Mr. Dunbar. I appreciate that."

"It's true. Have you thought about what you want to study in college?"

"Right now, I'm thinking about majoring in biomedical engineering and going to medical school."

"That's interesting. Why?"

That was the first weird part. I'm not used to adults asking me why after I say I want to major in engineering and go to med school. They usually just say that's awesome and keep it moving. I've gotten so used to that answer being enough to impress adults that I've never had to give it much more thought. I honestly don't know why.

"Well, I guess because I'm pretty good at science, and I feel like I should use that as a doctor to help people."

"Okay. I understand that. I just asked because I would say that your writing and research skills could also be used to help people in any number of fields."

"Thanks. I guess I never thought about it like that."

"It's true. I would encourage you to really think about how you want to put your skills to use. Being a doctor is a fine choice as well if that's what you decide. I just encourage you to explore your options."

"Thanks. I'll do that."

"You're welcome. On another note, I'm chaperoning a trip that the SGA is sponsoring to Chicago for spring break, and I'd love to have you join us if you can get permission from your parents. We'll get to tour city hall as well as a number of other sites around the city like the DuSable Museum of African American History."

"That would be awesome. I'll talk to my folks about it tonight."

"Great. You already know Harold's Chicken Shack is on the agenda, so you'll finally get to try it for yourself."

Thankfully my excitement about the trip helped me resist the urge to roll my eyes, and I said, "Sure. Why not? I'll give it a shot."

I was so caught up in thinking about the trip that I didn't notice Mr. Dunbar holding a book out toward me until it almost hit me in the chest.

"That's all I ask. On another note, I'd also like to give you this as an early graduation present. Are you familiar with Zora Neale Hurston?"

"Yes, sir. We talked about *Their Eyes Were Watching God* in Ms. Crenshaw's lit class last year."

"Yes. That's a wonderful read. This book was one of Hurston's final works and was published after her death. It's called *Barracoon: The Story of the Last 'Black Cargo.'* It tells the story of a man who was one of the last living formerly enslaved Africans who was actually transported to an area right outside Mobile. He is a member of the Yoruba tribe as well. "

"Thanks, Mr. Dunbar. I'll definitely read it."

"Anytime, Lewis. Hurston was a gifted writer and researcher as well. One of my favorite quotes of hers is 'Research is formalized curiosity. It is poking and prying with a purpose.' I find that to be true, and I hope you find the book helpful as you set out to determine what you want to do next."

"Thanks. I really appreciate it."

"You're welcome. Have a good evening, and let me know what your parents say about the trip," Mr. Dunbar said.

"Will do."

That thirty minutes with Mr. Dunbar was the first time since we lost to Parker that thinking about the future has made me smile, and I've got to thank him for that.

Chapter 4

Grandma Jean's the closest family member I've had to pass away, and I'm still getting used to the fact that she's not here anymore. I just realized the other day that I still have her number in my phone. Before starting this project, I just called her Grandma. I knew Jean was her name, but there was no need for an additional descriptor because she was the only Grandma—or grandparent for that matter—I'd known.

I thought that would make finishing her part of the project easier, but I'm realizing it's not that simple. We talked about a lot of things, but trying to piece it all together without having her here is more complicated than I thought.

One thing I do remember is something she said in what ended up being one of our last conversations: "Always remember that determination—not desire— determines your destiny." For some reason that stuck with me as soon as she said it. I even took my phone out and wrote it in my notes.

This was before our family even knew she was sick, so it wasn't like I had an idea of what the next few months would bring, and our conversation that day wasn't about anything particularly deep. Another topic I vividly remember laughing with her about that day was how fine she was back in her "heathen" days. Other than that, we were just catching up and talking about plans she had to do some renovations around the house when spring came.

Maybe Grandma's words that day stood out because they represented something about her personality that I can't really put into words, but I know it when I see it. It's the same feeling I get whenever I hear Jalen Rose, my favorite member of the Fab Five, talk about growing up in Detroit. I remember one episode of his podcast where he was interviewing Big Sean, and they talked about how Detroiters always find a way to survive, and not only survive, but to boss up too.

I wish I had talked to Grandma more about how life was for her when she was younger, but I do know that it wasn't easy. I learned from Mom that after high school, Grandma worked multiple odd jobs at a time to try to support the family. It was always Grandma's dream to teach one day though, and she eventually went back to college after all her children had grown up and got her degree in education. She was still teaching at Norwood Elementary up until right before she got sick.

As I thought about how to make up for the questions I never got to ask Grandma, my mind immediately went to Mrs. Lamar. She's a retired history teacher who goes to my church, and although she didn't know Grandma, they were around the same age and both from Birmingham. Plus, she's just one of the nicest ladies ever.

Mrs. Lamar's house isn't far from ours, and I've known her for as long as I can remember. Mom and Dad would always run to the store for her when we were younger, and they usually would have me and Ìfẹ́ with them so we'd inevitably end up staying over for a while so they could talk. Once I got old enough to drive, I started making the runs for her when my parents were busy, and now I always end up staying longer than expected too. Mrs. Lamar is just good people, and I figured this project would be right up her alley.

I gave her a call after my last class of the day to see if she needed anything from the store, and she said she needed some bread, so I stopped to get it before heading to her house. She was standing at the door waiting for me by the time I opened my car door.

"Hey there, Lewis. Thank you for running to the store for me. How much do I owe you?"

"You don't owe me anything Mrs. Lamar. It's no problem."

"Well thank you sugar. Come on in the house at least and let me get you something to drink. Is chamomile tea alright?"

"Yes, Ma'am that would be perfect. Thank you."

As we talked, I followed Mrs. Lamar to her kitchen. She filled two glasses of tea for us, and we both sat down at the kitchen table. Right before taking my first sip, I asked, "How have you been doing?"

"I'm doing fine. Just waiting on this weather to warm up so I can get out to my garden. How are your parents doing?"

"They're doing well."

"That's good. Make sure you tell them I said hello."

"I will."

"And that gorgeous sister of yours?"

"She's fine."

"Well, that's wonderful. Tell her to get over here and see me soon. How are you doing though, baby? How's school?"

"Yes, ma'am, I will. I'm good though, and school is going well. I actually wanted to talk to you about a class project I could use your help with."

"I'd love to help. What do you need?"

"I'm trying to better understand what Birmingham was like when my grandma was coming up, and I thought it would be great to talk to you since you're from the city, too, and y'all were about the same age."

"Okay, well, I'll do everything I can to help. What year was your grandmother born?"

"In 1940."

"Was she really? I knew from talking to your mother that we were close in age, but I didn't know it was that close. I was born in 1939, so I'm certain we knew some of the same people. I know your mother is from Collegeville. Is that where your grandmother was reared too?

"Yes, ma'am. My great-grandparents moved to Birmingham from a small town in Georgia when she was a baby, but she grew up in Collegeville."

"Okay then. Well, Lewis, one of the first things you need to understand is that Collegeville was a factory town. Almost everyone that lived there around the time your grandmother was born would have had some connection to the plants and factories in North Birmingham, whether it was U.S. Pipe, L&N Railroad, or ACIPCO. The working conditions on those jobs were difficult and often hazardous, but it was honest work and allowed you to support a family. The next thing you need to know is that around the time your grandmother was born, the country was just beginning to fully recover from the Depression, and nowhere in the country had it worse than Birmingham."

"Really?"

"Yes, sugar. It was terrible. President Roosevelt said it himself that Birmingham was the 'worst hit town in the country.' People had lost everything, and that was across the board, but like I always tell y'all, when America gets the sniffles, black folk get pneumonia, so you can imagine what it was like for us."

We both laughed because that's one of Mrs. Lamar's favorite sayings. She and Grandma Jean definitely would have been friends because they have the same sense of humor.

"It's the truth. So, you have to realize that's the world we were born into. The country was just starting to bounce back thanks to the New Deal programs from the government, but our folk weren't given equal access to those either, so can you see how our recovery would have still been a few steps behind?"

"Yes, ma'am."

"Alright then, so right around that same time, the country goes to war, and our world is turned upside down again. The war lasted from 1939 to 1945, so this would have been the first five years of your grandmother's life, and it affected everybody in some way. Daddy served with the 761st Tank Battalion in France, but almost every family on our street had someone go off to war. Do you know if any of your grandmother's people were in the service?"

"I don't know. I know my mom's dad fought in the Korean War, but I'll have to ask my mom about World War II."

"Yes, sugar. You need to ask her. Around this time, you also had a lot of black families that decided to leave the South altogether. My Aunt Johnnie and Uncle Buck moved up to Michigan in 1942. Uncle Buck got a job at the Willow Run manufacturing plant making bomber jets for the military, and Aunt Johnnie found work teaching at Miller High School in Detroit. My cousins and their children have been living up there ever since."

"We learned in school about how a lot of black people moved up north and out west because there were more job opportunities."

"Yes, sugar, there were more job opportunities available, but the real reason most people left was because they didn't feel like they could safely raise a family down here."

"Really?"

"Yes. It was a dangerous time to be black in the South, not that it's ever been easy anywhere, but it could be especially terrifying here. Growing up, we lived right off 20th Street in Ensley, and when I was a little girl, the Birmingham Police Department and the Klan paraded right down our street one night."

I paused for a second as I tried to make sure I understood what Mrs. Lamar had just said. I figured I couldn't have heard her right. "Did you say the police and the Klan were together?"

"Like Smokey Robinson and the Miracles. The only reason you could tell where one ended and the other began was because of the white hoods. Just think about it: This was the busiest street in a community that they knew was heavily populated by blacks, so it wasn't an accident. They were sending a message, and we heard it loud and clear."

"Wow. Do you know why y'all didn't move?"

"I honestly don't. I never asked, and Mama and Daddy never brought up moving. Of course, we saw families all around us leaving, but I guess Mama and Daddy just decided we were here to stay. I can't imagine having left now. Birmingham is the only place I've ever lived other than the four years I was at Tuskegee."

Another thing to know about Mrs. Lamar is that she loves Tuskegee University. She was actually wearing a Tuskegee crewneck while I was interviewing her.

"I never thought to ask you before, but how did you know Tuskegee was the right school for you? Did you always want to go there?"

"Honestly, what led me to Tuskegee was one of my teachers at Holy Family High School, Mrs. Richardson. She was a member of our church and a good friend of my mother's. Mama and Daddy didn't have the opportunity to go to college, but they were committed to making sure I went, and they asked Mrs. Richardson to tutor me. Over time, I would always hear Mrs. Richardson talk about how much she had enjoyed her time at Tuskegee, and I admired her so much that when it came time for me to choose a school, I couldn't think of anywhere else I'd rather go. Then I think it made Mama and Daddy comfortable to know they had someone who had been there before and could help me get situated. Out of all the years I knew Mrs. Richardson, the happiest I've ever seen her other than when I got baptized was when I told her I was going to Tuskegee."

Mrs. Lamar and I both laughed, and we talked for a little while more before I thanked her and headed home. Talking to Mrs. Lamar really helped me fill in a lot of gaps about things that Grandma Jean might have experienced when she was younger. It was cool to hear Mrs. Lamar talk about her old teacher too. I could tell that those were good memories for her. After our conversation, I really like the direction the project is going.

All that's left to do now is fill in a lifetime of gaps and missed conversations with the grandma I never got to meet.

Chapter 5

They say a picture is worth a thousand words, and since pictures are all I have of Grandma Ìfẹ́, I try to get as much out of them as possible. There's one picture in particular that always comes to mind whenever I think of her. It's from the last time she and my granddad visited the United States a few months after my parents got married. Mom, Dad, and Granddad are all in the picture, too, but Grandma Ìfẹ́ is right in the middle, so your eye is immediately drawn to her.

The name *Ìfẹ́* means love. *Ìfẹ́* was also the name of the first kingdom of the Yoruba people, and now there are more than thirty-five million Yorubas in Nigeria and even more around the world.

I knew right away that talking to Dad was a must to prepare for the Grandma Ìfẹ́ portion of the project. Every year in elementary school, whenever a new teacher heard his accent, they'd ask him to come speak to our class about Nigeria, and he always said yes. It was actually kind of cool. Dad's pretty low-key, but he gets excited when he really cares about something and can be pretty interesting.

I talk a lot about Mom and how serious she is about academics, but Dad is just as serious. He's just more laid-back by nature. If our family were a band, Mom would be the drummer because she's going to instantly grab your attention whenever she steps on the scene. Ìfẹ́ would be on the saxophone because she always has a cool demeanor, regardless of what's going on around her. I'd be on the trumpet, not because of any particular personality trait. I just remember seeing Mom's favorite actor Denzel Washington playing it in an old movie she was watching, and he made it look good. But anyway, Dad would be on the bass guitar. He may not be the flashiest, but if he weren't there, you would notice it right away because the sound would be off. He sets

the tone that allows everybody else to play their role at a
high level.

Dad tells us stories about growing up all the time,
and we attend Nigerian functions pretty regularly, but
I've never asked much about his parents. The two times
he's been back to Nigeria since I was born were for their
funerals, and I was too young to remember anything
other than waving bye from the car seat when we
dropped him off at the airport. I'm actually excited to
learn more about what Grandma Ìfẹ́ was like, and I figure
it may bring up some good memories for Dad too.

This morning while he was getting ready for work,
I asked Dad what time would be good for me to interview
him, and he said we could do it right after dinner. So,
Dad and I just stayed at the table after we got done
eating while Mom and Ìfẹ́ went to the beauty supply
store. Mr. Dunbar mentioned that it would be a good
idea to have some questions prepared beforehand to
help guide the conversation, and he recommended

recording the interviews with our phones to make sure we don't miss anything. So, as soon as I set the phone down and pressed record, I started with my first question.

"When was Grandma born?"

"Mom was born in 1931."

"Did she ever talk to you about what it was like for her growing up?"

"She spoke positively of her upbringing. I learned later that she was born during a time of financial peril due to the Great Depression, but she never spoke of any specific troubles because that was not her nature."

"The Great Depression affected Nigeria too? I always thought it was just an American thing."

"Oh no. It was an international crisis. Do you remember what I told you about the global financial markets being interconnected and how what affects one will inevitably affect the others? It is as the proverb says,

'Bí ó bá bá ojú, á bá imú pèlú'— 'Whatever disaster befalls the eye will also befall the nose.'"

Dad's an accountant, and he's always talking to me about money and the stock market, so he has mentioned that before. Another important thing to note about Dad is that he loves speaking in proverbs.

"I do remember you mentioning that."

"Nigeria was still being colonized by the British at that time. We did not gain independence until 1960. Britain's economy was ravaged by the Depression, and Nigeria, along with their other colonies, was forced to bear the brunt of the damage."

"Oh, wow."

"Yes, they were trying times."

"Where was her hometown?"

"Her ancestral village is called Idi Aga. It is about twenty-five miles away from my dad's hometown, Ilaro, which is where our family home in Nigeria is. They are both located in Abeokuta, which is the capital of Ogun

State in Southwest Nigeria. For comparison, if Ogun State were Alabama, Abeokuta would be Montgomery, and Ilaro and Idi Aga would be neighborhoods in the area."

"Okay. How did she and Granddad meet?"

"Well, as a young man, my dad was a locomotive train conductor. That is where he says he got the call to ministry. He says it was around Christmas when people were singing Christmas carols. I remember that carol was…it will come to me…'It Came Upon a Midnight Clear.' That was the title of the song, and my dad said he just felt the call to go into ministry. So shortly thereafter, he went to teach in the village at the Baptist Day School. The school was located in Idi Aga, and he met Mom while traveling through the village. They were married not long after that, and then he went to seminary for his formal training as a minister."

"Is the school he taught at the one that Grandma would have gone to growing up?"

"If not that one specifically, then it would have been somewhere similar. Abeokuta was where the first Christian missionary base in the land of the Yorubas was established around the 1840s. It was common practice that whenever missionaries established a base of operation that they would open a school not long after. The purposes were twofold: to instruct the children in terms of Christian discipleship and to provide academic training. The missionaries knew how important education was to our people, and they sought to build connection through providing schooling. Mom attended school up through what would be considered middle school in America, but after that, she began working, and my dad attended up through university."

"Where did Granddad go to college?"

"He initially attended Baptist Theological Seminary in Ogbomoso, a city in Oyo State, which borders Ogun State to the north, and his first pastoral appointment was in Kumasi, Ghana. That is what led him and Mom to move to Ghana while I was an infant."

"I didn't know that. I knew you lived in Ghana before, but I thought it was when you were older."

"Yes, we were in Ghana from when I was a year old until I was twelve. All of my siblings were actually born there. I can still speak the dialect of the Ashanti tribe, but I am not as fluent as I once was. Dad pastored at the church in Kumasi for eleven years, and then he went to Southeastern Baptist Theological Seminary in Winston-Salem, North Carolina, where he received his diploma in theology."

"Oh, wow. So Grandma was there with all five of you? How long was Granddad in the U.S.?"

"He completed his studies in two-and-a-half years and then returned. Mom was accustomed to managing the household because Dad's work as a pastor required regular travel, even when he was home. She was skilled in agriculture, so she harvested millet, a type of grain, and raised chickens. She used the income from that, as well as the money Dad sent back every month, to provide for us. Yoruba women are known for being industrious and highly skilled at trading in the marketplace, and Mom was no different. She had been working since she was a youth when she first began as a porter."

"What are porters?"

"Porters are people that carry burdens. Have you seen the pictures of people from back home carrying items on their heads?"

"Yes, I've seen those."

"Those people are 'portering' or transporting those items from one place to another. Sometimes it may be for their own personal household, but it is often as a form of commerce."

"Oh, okay. Why did you all leave Ghana?"

"We left Ghana when the president then, Busia, made a decree that all aliens should go back to their country. We call it the deportation order. About two hundred thousand people, more than half of whom were Yoruba, were given two weeks to leave the country."

"Really? How could they call you aliens when you'd been there since you were one and all of your siblings were born there?"

"They did not care to take that into account. They considered us aliens based on the fact that our parents were born in Nigeria. Ghana's economy was suffering, and during such times, it is easy for fearful leaders to alienate anyone who is different. Unfortunately, Nigerian leaders resorted to the same tactic years later, forcing two million migrants, half of whom were Ghanaians, to leave the country or face arrest. This was seen by many as payback, but it only weakened the relations between our countries, and unfortunately, negative feelings still linger for some. It is sad because prior to the arrival of the Europeans, Africans did not traditionally view borders in that way because of our shared ancestry. I thankfully still consider many Ghanaians my friends, but we often lament how our countries have allowed borders set in place by colonizers to affect our relations with one another."

"Oh, wow. Do you remember what it was like when you all had to leave?"

"I remember very well talking to my mother around that time. The house we grew up in was split level, made of wood, and I was sitting in my mother's bedroom by the window… Because back then…just like I'm talking to you now, when we were growing up…our dad…you don't have casual talk with your dad. It's only with Mom, all the time. It wasn't due to a lack of love on Dad's part, but Mom was often the one we went to with questions during challenging times.

A common name that the Igbo tribe gives to their children back home is Nneka, and it means 'Mother is Supreme'. The meaning is that when the circumstances of life become overwhelming, a child—even once they've become an adult—will often seek comfort from their mother. That is why mothers always hold a supreme place in the hearts of their children.

When the deportation order forced our family to move back to Nigeria, Mom reassured us that we would be fine, and we believed her. She did the same for me years later when I was preparing to come to this country to attend Campbell University. As the time drew near for me to leave, I was worried whether or not I had made the right decision in choosing to come to America for school. Mom sensed my anxiety and comforted me by praying with me and reminding me that Campbell was in North Carolina where Dad had already established friendships with people who would be able to watch out for me."

"Was Grandad the reason you chose to go to college in North Carolina?"

"Yes. In addition to the connections he had, he would always talk about how beautiful North Carolina was."

As Dad was talking, I heard Mom and Ìfẹ́ walk back in the house, which surprised me because they usually spend at least an hour in the beauty supply store. I didn't pay it much attention because I was focused on listening to Dad. But right as he had finished talking about North Carolina, Ìfẹ́ came and sat down next to him and said, "So, have you asked about how Mom and Dad met yet?"

Dad laughed, and I rolled my eyes and said, "No, I haven't. That's not what the project is about. Aren't you supposed to be getting your hair done?"

"Mom's getting set up, so I figured I would join y'all," Ìfẹ́ said, smiling. "When are you going to interview me?"

I gave Ìfẹ́ a confused look as I replied, "Uh, never."

Then she said "Why not? I'm named after Grandma, and Dad always says she and I have a lot in common. Remember, Dad, it's like the proverb you told us about being like our ancestors. I think it was *Ipa abẹ́rẹ́ lokùn ńtọ̀*—it is the path blazed by the needle that the thread follows."

"Great job, Ìfẹ́!" Dad said as he reached over and gave her a hug. "I can tell that you have been practicing your Yoruba. Your sister is right, Lewis. She does share many traits with your grandmother."

Smiling from ear to ear and content that she had proven her point, Ìfẹ́ said, "Thanks, Dad" as she stood from the table. As she passed me on her way out of the kitchen, she looked at me and said, "I'll be ready whenever you are."

One thing I've gotta give Ìfẹ́ is that she knows how to make a good argument. That's why she wants to go to law school—well that and her obsession with being like Michelle Obama. After my talk with Dad, I can see why he would say that she's like Grandma in a lot of ways.

I'm still not interviewing her though.

Chapter 6

Working on my Capstone interviews has taken up so much of my time that it almost made me forget about the fact that I still don't have any basketball scholarship offers yet.

Almost.

I still think about it every day, but with me being so busy, I've been able to push it to the back of my mind. After completing that portion of the project last night with Dad, all that's left now is to work on my presentation.

I know I should be happy because in addition to the project going well, Mom and Dad have given me the okay to go on the Chicago trip with Mr. Dunbar and the SGA. I still woke up this morning feeling depressed though. It's like the weight of the season being over and having no offers has hit me all over again.

It's well known in our house that whenever I'm in my feelings, the one place you can find me is downstairs in the family room watching Giannis Antetokounmpo's acceptance speech from when he won his first NBA Most Valuable Player award. Giannis has been my favorite player ever since Dad told me that his last name means "the crown has returned from overseas" in Yoruba.

You would think with me having seen the speech so many times that it would lose its effect, but it never does. I can almost quote it word for word, and sometimes I'll catch myself saying it while I'm watching it. Everyone in the house loves the speech, too, and sometimes I can tell they're in the back watching it with me and just don't want to interrupt, except for Ìfẹ́. She usually will just come sit right next to me on the couch.

I'm usually the earliest riser in the house on the weekends, so with everything that was on my mind, I washed up, threw on a yellow Michigan t-shirt, navy blue sweats, and my Michigan hat for additional good vibes, and headed downstairs. I figured the speech would help me clear my head before everyone else woke up. The speech is about six minutes long, and I was at the halfway mark when I heard someone walking down the steps. I was surprised because of how early it was that anyone else would be awake, but I was so locked in on the speech that I didn't bother turning around. As I heard the steps getting closer to the couch, I knew it was Ìfẹ́. She grabbed a blanket and sat down next to me right as Giannis started to thank his family.

Giannis starts by thanking his late father. He talks about how he always thinks of his dad whenever he steps on the court and how that motivates him to work hard even when he doesn't feel like it. Then he thanks his brothers for being his role models and talks about how he looks up to them.

The final member of his family that Giannis thanks is his mom. He starts off by calling his mom his hero, and then he talks about how "when you're a little kid, you don't see the future…but if you have a good parent, your parent sees the future for you." Then he thanks his mom for how she always saw the future for him and his brothers. After that, Giannis wraps up by thanking his agents and then says that winning the MVP award was just the beginning and how his goal was to win a championship, which he went on to do not long after. It's just a great speech, and as usual, after listening to it, I feel a little better.

I'd smiled at Ìfẹ́ when she sat down on the couch, but neither of us had said anything while the speech was on. She broke the silence once the speech ended by asking me, "So, what brings you to Giannis today?"

I laughed and said, "I was just feeling a little down about my scholarship situation."

"I don't understand. You get letters from colleges every day."

"Those aren't for basketball though, Ìfẹ́."

"Okay, but it's still people who will pay for your school. Can't you just try out for the team when you get there?"

"Technically, but it's not like high school. There are only so many spots available for people that aren't on scholarship."

"But you would be on scholarship."

"I'd be on an academic scholarship, not a basketball one."

"Same difference. This reminds me of something I heard last week on *Therapy for Black Girls*. It sounds like you're seeking unnecessary validation. You should listen to the episode."

"I would, but there's just the thing about me not being a black girl," I said as I chuckled.

Ìfẹ́ rolled her eyes and said, "Whatever, Lewis. Instead of worrying about getting Granddad's height, you need to be hoping that you inherit his fashion sense. You know God made other colors outside of blue and yellow, right, and when are you gonna let that hat go?"

As she was talking, she reached over in an attempt to knock my hat off, but I caught her hand right in time, which led to a mini-wrestling session between us. I was so busy trying to keep Ìfẹ́'s hand away from my head that I didn't even notice Mom was in the room until I heard her say, "Y'all cut it out before you break something you can't afford—like everything."

At that point, Ìfẹ́ got up from the couch and began to head upstairs. As she was walking by me she said, "Okay, Lewis. Keep the hat. If you want to spend the rest of your life dressed like a Walmart employee, that's on you. Mom, I wouldn't hold my breath on getting grandkids from this one."

I rolled my eyes and dodged her predictable last attempt to knock the hat over before she left the room. Once Ìfẹ́ was gone, Mom came and sat next to me on the couch.

"You know your sister's right, Lewis."

"Really, Mom?" I said in disbelief.

"I'm talking about school, not that other foolishness. I always tell you how handsome you are. I'm saying that you should be just as proud of those academic scholarships as you would any basketball scholarship."

I didn't even know Mom had heard that part of the conversation. How long had she been standing there?

"I know, Mom. I guess doing well at school has always come naturally, so it just feels different."

"Just because it comes natural to you doesn't mean it comes natural to everyone. You've got a gift, son, and it was given to you for a reason. You're more than just an athlete. Much more."

"I know, Mom. Thanks."

"Do you want to know why I didn't send you to play for that coach in Arkansas?" Mom said, referring to the basketball coach who'd guaranteed he could get me a Division I scholarship offer back when I was in middle school.

"Why?"

"Because I could tell that all he saw in you was what you could do for him. Your father and I have known since you and Ìfẹ́ were babies that you're both bright enough to get academic scholarships. You still have to put in the work, but we know you have the potential. Our responsibility as your parents is to help you reach that potential. Do you understand?"

"Yes, ma'am."

"Y'all aren't our early retirement plan. We just love you. But so many of these coaches only care about you for as long as you can produce for them. There are some good ones out there, but even they aren't meant to play the role of your parents. That's our job. So when it came to sports, your dad and I agreed early on that we would stay in our lane and make sure that every coach stayed in theirs. I told that coach no because you didn't need him. I knew you could get a scholarship on your own, but there were some things that you did need as a teenage black boy that only your father and I could provide, and we couldn't do that while you were four hundred miles away in Arkansas. Do you understand?"

"Yes, ma'am. I understand."

"Good. Now go tell your sister you're sorry. She was clearly just trying to help you."

"Mom? How is telling me I dress like a Walmart employee help?"

"She only went there after you ignored her advice. What can I say? She's like her mother. Her love may come wrapped differently, but it's love all the same. You know that."

"Yes, ma'am."

"Good. Now y'all work that out while I run to the store for Mrs. Lamar and then over to see your aunt Ruth. I'll be back in time for dinner."

I walked in yesterday on Mom and Dad talking about Aunt Ruth's cancer being back, and they told me they didn't want me and Ìfẹ́ to worry. I'm trying to stay positive because I know she beat cancer a couple years ago, but I overheard Mom telling Dad it's a more aggressive form this time. The doctors apparently caught it early though, so I'm praying that Aunt Ruth will be okay.

"Yes, ma'am. How is Aunt Ruth doing?"

"She's doing okay. Just working with the doctors on what the plan for treatment is going to be this time around. I'm just going over to spend some time with her. Make sure you give her a call before your trip to Chicago. She was excited to hear that you're going. You know she lived in Chicago for a while after college."

"Really? I didn't know that. I'll make sure to call her. Please tell her and Mrs. Lamar I said hey."

"I will. I love you, Lewis."

"I love you too, Mom."

I know Mom's right that I should be just as proud of an academic scholarship, but I just never really looked at school and basketball the same way. I've always known school was important, but I've never really had to study to do well. Mom says I get my memory from Dad and that we only need to hear or see something once and then we remember it forever. That plus paying attention has always been enough to keep me near the top of my class.

The only exception is math. Ever since math began involving letters and numbers, we haven't seen eye to eye. Seriously though, pre-calculus last year was the hardest I've ever had to work for a B. There was one point where I really felt like giving up but talking to Aunt Ruth helped me make it through.

Aunt Ruth is great at math. She graduated at the top of her class at Parker, got her undergrad degree in math at the University of Miami, and then her master's at the University of Michigan. Now she's a computer programmer. Mom told me to reach out to her when I was having trouble and that convo has changed the way I look at math ever since.

"Lewis, you're letting yourself get too discouraged when you get a question wrong. Getting it wrong is part of getting it right in math. It doesn't mean you're a failure or that you're not smart. It's all a part of the process of making you better. It's just a different process than you're used to because your memory has always been enough to get you through. Math doesn't test your memory as much as it does your strategy, and the only way to master math is through practice, which is going to require a lot of wrong answers along the way. You just have to embrace that part of the process."

Ever since then, I've looked at math differently. It's still not easy by any means, but I don't expect it to be anymore, and I embrace the challenge. I can still get down on myself sometimes, but thinking about what Aunt Ruth said gets me back on track.

I've been worried about Mom since I found out about Aunt Ruth being sick because I know how close they are, but Mom seems to be doing well. I'm still trying to make sure I don't add any unnecessary stress to her though. For that reason only, I'll apologize to Ìfẹ́ , and I'll never admit it but that Walmart line was actually pretty funny.

Chapter 7

It's the Friday before spring break, and we're out of school today. Some people say the reason we get this day off is because all the seniors used to be absent anyway for Senior Skip Day. I never asked if that's true or not because I don't need an explanation for an off day. I'm the only person at the house for the next few hours because Mom and Dad are at work, and I just dropped Ìfẹ́ off at dance team practice.

I'm hoping to use the time to myself to work on ideas for my Capstone presentation, but I keep drawing blanks. Capstone Day is only a few weeks after we get back from spring break, so it's definitely crunch time. I've found that my most creative ideas come when I'm working out and listening to music, so I grab my laptop and head down to the garage.

I've got one workout playlist on YouTube with like a million videos on it. There's gospel, naija, R&B, trap, and everything else in between. Ìfẹ́ is way more organized and has her playlists broken down by themes. She listens to "specific songs to create specific vibes". Music in itself is a vibe for me though, and the way I see it, my playlist has something for any mood, so, in a way, you could say it's more efficient. Ìfẹ́ would disagree, but that's cool. We just have creative differences—I'm creative, and she's different.

I'm joking. Her playlists are actually dope. It's just too much work to run back and forth to the laptop mid-workout whenever I need a change of pace, so we agree to disagree.

As soon as I get down to the garage and open up the blinds to let the light in, I instantly start feeling good. I let my playlist go, and I jump right into my workout. After about ten minutes, I'm in a zone until "Higher" with Nipsey Hussle, DJ Khaled, and John Legend comes on.

That song has always been one of my favorites because Nipsey mentions his dad coming from Africa in the first verse. That instantly made me want to look more into him, and I learned that his dad came from Eritrea as a teenager, and he met his mom in California. Even though I'd obviously never met Nipsey, it was cool to know we had something in common.

So given that and the fact that "Higher" was Nipsey's last video, I thought I was just experiencing the same nostalgic vibes I always get when I listen to it. But this was the first time I'd heard it since I started working on my Capstone project, and the line about his grandma hit differently than before. In the verse he talks about how his grandma had miscarriages every year for almost ten years before she gave birth to his mom. This is the first time I've thought about that from his grandma's—I'm sorry Ms. Margaret Boutte's—point of view.

Mr. Dunbar talked to us the other day about how the project should help us to recognize women as individuals instead of just through how they're connected to us.

Before I know it, I've put the weights down, and I'm looking for as much information about Ms. Boutte as I can find. I start with a Rap Genius interview where Nipsey talked about the backstory behind the verse. He talked about how Ms. Boutte had thirteen pregnancies and has two kids—his uncle and his mom. The story of her pregnancy history was one that she would often tell her family, saying things like, "Imagine if I would have given up on my ninth or tenth miscarriage."

Nipsey said he would always hear the stories, but for some reason one day it hit him that if she had given up, then he wouldn't have ever been born.

At this point, I'm so caught up in her story that I'm not even thinking of the project until I come across an article he wrote for *The Players' Tribune* called "For the Culture." Nipsey talked about how in a neighborhood with actual gangsters, his grandma was tougher than all of them. It stood out to me that he said, "Her preferred weapon was a type of love and calm that was so big, it could consume the toughest OG."

One of the benefits of reading a lot is that I never really forget things I read. I may not have them at the top of my mind all the time, but all it takes is for something to trigger my memory, and it all starts coming back to me. As soon as I read that part about his grandma's "preferred weapon" being love, I knew I'd seen that somewhere before.

So I run up to our bookshelf and start thumbing through all the books until I find it. It's *Strength to Love* by Dr. Martin Luther King, Jr. We had to read it last year for school, and I always underline things that stand out, so it doesn't take me long to find what I'm looking for: *"In a world depending on force, coercive tyranny, and bloody violence, you are challenged to follow the way of love. You will then discover that unarmed love is the most powerful force in all the world."*

Strength to Love stuck with me because it was the first time I felt like I really got to understand MLK's thought process. It taught me that he didn't choose love because of fear, but because he actually believed it was the better way. He takes the time to explain why he thought nonviolence motivated by love was the most effective method, and ultimately the conclusion he comes to is that love's ability to persevere even when things are hard is what makes it so powerful.

Mr. Dunbar told us to look for common threads in our research to help us as we prepare our presentations. He explained that common threads are "recurring ideas or principles that your audience will be able to clearly recognize and relate to," and I feel like perseverance may be a common thread for me. Grandma Jean and Grandma Ìfẹ́ had different experiences but having to persevere through challenging circumstances is something that they both have in common.

As I'm thinking of how to express that through my presentation, my phone rings. It's Aunt Ruth.

"Hey, Aunt Ruth. How are you doing?"

"I'm doing well, Lewis. I'm just calling to check on you. I hear you've got a trip to Chicago coming up."

"I do. I was actually planning on calling you soon because Mom said you used to live up there."

"I did. Many, many moons ago. I'm excited for you. When do you all leave?"

"Our flight leaves Monday, so I've got a couple days."

"Okay. Are you busy tomorrow morning?"

"I'm not. What's up?"

"I was wondering if you might be available to run an errand with me. I'm heading to Wedowee and just figured some company might be nice for an early morning drive. I just need to stop by one place in particular and then head on back. We can get lunch on the way back."

“Of course. I'm down to go.”

“Great. This will be just like the road trips me and your mom used to make, except I'm sure you may not want to listen to Anita Baker the whole way.”

“Aye, I've got love for Anita. I wouldn't be mad at that.”

“Well alright then! I'll swing by to pick you up around nine.”

“Sounds good. I'll see you then.”

“Alright, Lewis. I love you.”

“I love you too.”

Chapter 8

Wedowee, Alabama, is about an hour and a half from Birmingham heading east toward Atlanta. It's pronounced *wee-dow-wee,* and I learned from Aunt Ruth growing up that it means "old water" in the language of the Creek tribe of Native Americans that used to live here. Of all the places in the "country" that our family visits, this is the one we've been to most, usually to visit family that used to live out here. The population is around eight hundred people, so it's not big enough to have its own exit, but about twenty minutes after you get off the interstate, you run right into it.

It's crazy the things you don't think about when you're traveling as a little kid, but I never noticed how much bluer the sky is here. It's definitely a place where you can see all the stars at night. I'll always be a city kid, but I can't deny that it's beautiful out here.

Aunt Ruth didn't mention where exactly we're going in Wedowee, so I just go with the flow. We stopped for a restroom break and to get gas once we made it into town, and Aunt Ruth and I shared a laugh at the sign on the front door of the gas station.

WARNING

THIS ESTABLISHMENT IS POLITICALLY INCORRECT

WE SAY MERRY CHRISTMAS

GOD BLESS AMERICA

WE SALUTE OUR TROOPS AND OUR FLAG

IF THIS OFFENDS YOU

WE ARE NOT SORRY

Once we got back in the car, we drove for a couple more minutes before pulling into the parking lot of a place called Flat Rock Park, according to the sign. I've never been here before, but it looks like a nice park. There's a play area for kids, spots to picnic and fish, and a trail that leads down to Lake Wedowee. While I've never been to this park, I do remember Lake Wedowee because the cousins that we used to visit here had a house out by the lake.

Other than a group of guys fishing a couple hundred yards away, there is no one else out here but me and Aunt Ruth. As we get out of the car, Aunt Ruth asks me to grab the two lawn chairs from the back of the car. After following her down the trail to a spot a few feet away from the lake, I set the chairs down.

The first thing I notice once I look up from setting the chairs down is the view. The lake stretches out for miles on either side of us, so picture-perfect blue water is all we see to our left or right. The straight-ahead view offers more of the same, with the only addition being little islands with the greenest grass I've ever seen sprinkled in between. I already talked about how much bluer the sky is here, but as I look around, I'm realizing the color quality of everything feels enhanced.

As we both took our seats, Aunt Ruth said, "This lake is beautiful, isn't it?"

I nodded my head and said, "It is. I forgot how nice it was out here."

Then she laughed and said, "I feel like it was just yesterday that you and Ìfẹ́ were out here running around, and now I can't believe you're both almost grown…Y'all used to remind me of coming out here when I was a little girl…" Aunt Ruth paused for a moment and sighed as she looked out over the lake before starting again, "and how Mom always insisted that we spend as much time out by the lake as possible."

Aunt Ruth's mom was my Great-Aunt Irene. She passed away a few years ago, but I have a ton of great memories of her and my other great-aunts coming to Wedowee with us every summer. Spending time with them was always fun because they would tell me funny stories about how I was as a baby and how much I reminded them of Grandad Lewis.

"I was eight years old when I finally asked Mom what it was about the lake that was so special to her, and I still remember her smiling and asking me if I knew what it meant to have my soul restored," Aunt Ruth said, laughing. "As I would assume is the case for any eight-year-old, I said no ma'am, and just when I thought she was going to explain it to me, she looked down at me and said, 'just keep living.'"

Aunt Ruth and I both laughed and then we just sat taking in the sights and sounds of the lake for what had to be at least ten minutes straight. It could have been longer, but I don't know for sure because I wasn't really concerned with the time. With a view like this, it's honestly hard to focus on anything else. When I took a second to glance over at Aunt Ruth, I could tell she was thinking the same thing, and that's when it hit me that maybe this feeling is why we came out here.

Eventually, Aunt Ruth broke the silence to ask about my Capstone project.

"So, your mom tells me that you've been working on a school project about your grandmothers. How is that going?"

"It's going really well," I told her. "I've learned a lot about both of them, and now I'm just trying to bring it all together for my presentation."

"That's wonderful," she said. "Your grandmothers were two phenomenal women. You know your grandma Jean is the reason your parents met?"

"Huh?" I said, forgetting my manners in the midst of my genuine surprise. "Sorry. I mean, how?"

"Jean was working as a sales associate at the same retail store where your dad was working as an accountant, and she overheard him talking about looking for an apartment in the area, so she offered to have him rent out one of the rooms upstairs in her house. Once your mother heard about it, she insisted that she meet this 'stranger' before Jean gave him a key and ended up getting herself killed. Jean agreed to have them meet, and once they did, they were both done for," Aunt Ruth said, smiling. "I still get tickled when I remember your mom telling me, 'Girl, I'd never met any tall Nigerians.'"

Aunt Ruth and I both laughed, and all I could think about was how hard Ìfẹ́ and I were going to laugh about that when I made it home.

What threw me for a loop was what Aunt Ruth said next though. "Now that I think about it, you were one of the main topics of discussion when Jean and your grandma Ìfẹ́ first met."

"Hold on. Are you saying Grandma Jean and Grandma Ìfẹ́ met before…and they talked about me?" I knew that Grandma Ìfẹ́ had been to the United States from the picture at home, but I guess I just mentally limited the people she'd spent time with to the people in the picture.

"Of course they did," Aunt Ruth said. "Your dad's parents weren't able to make it to your parents' wedding, but they came to visit as soon as they could, which ended up being about five months later. By that time your mom was pregnant with you, and everyone was so excited that it's all they could talk about."

It's hard to explain how hearing that made me feel. It was like confirmation that I never knew I needed. I didn't even realize that I was tearing up until Aunt Ruth leaned over and put her hand on my shoulder.

"Yes, they were very excited, and I know they're proud of the young man that you're becoming," Aunt Ruth said, smiling.

"Thanks," I said. "I really appreciate that."

"I appreciate you coming out here with me this morning," Aunt Ruth said as she stood from her chair to take one last gaze at the lake. "Now let's head on back. I owe you lunch, and you've got some packing to do."

Chapter 9

I was initially confused when Aunt Ruth recommended that I pack a jacket for the trip because in Birmingham it's only cold enough to wear a jacket from like Thanksgiving to around Valentine's Day, and even that's pushing it sometimes. But as soon as we touched down in Chicago, I was glad I listened to her. I looked at my phone to check the weather on the way to baggage claim, and when it said that the high for the day was going to be forty degrees, I immediately wondered if Chicago had gotten the memo that it's supposed to be March.

Weather aside, Chicago has been great though. I'm one of twelve students who came on the trip, and we have three chaperones, Mr. Dunbar and two parents. We've been able to see a lot during our time up here, but there are two places in particular that have been my favorites so far, and with Mr. Dunbar serving as the tour guide, I guess it's no surprise that they're both on the south side.

The first is the DuSable Museum of African American History. I love history in general, so all of the exhibits were great, but my favorite one was about the African American soldiers who fought in World War I. The museum guide leading our group talked to us about how the "taste of freedom" that the black soldiers experienced while they were fighting in France planted the seeds for the Civil Rights Movement in America. Mr. Dunbar talked about how the soldiers couldn't ignore the fact that they were on a mission to make the world safe for democracy overseas, only to come back and realize that they didn't have democracy at home.

My second favorite place was Simeon Academy. As a basketball fan, it's just a legendary place because it's where Derrick Rose went, and the gym is named after Ben Wilson, another alum and Chicago basketball legend. It turns out that Mr. Dunbar was an alum, too, and he even played ball up until his junior year when he decided to focus on track.

Going to Simeon wasn't originally on the agenda, but there was a free period where students could either head back to the hotel with one of the parent chaperones or to the mall with the other parent chaperone. Mr. Dunbar was actually planning to head to Simeon by himself to meet up with one of his old classmates, but he asked if I was interested in coming along once his friend mentioned an open run that was going on at the school gym if anyone from our group was interested in playing basketball. Of course I said yes, and we headed that way.

Needless to say, once we made it to the school, I wanted to make sure I held my own on the court. I noticed right away that it was a really competitive atmosphere, and that made me even more excited. Just judging by looks, everybody on the court was between high school age and early twenties. I ended up being teamed with four local guys. I was the tallest, but we had one other guy around six-two, and everybody else was between five-ten and six feet.

I clicked with our point guard right away. He introduced himself as Keyandre, but everybody called him Dre. I eventually picked up that he played high school ball at Simeon, and now he's playing college ball at Chicago State. Dre's around six feet with a smooth jumper out to three-point range and a nice handle, but what instantly stood out to me was his vision. His passes weren't necessarily flashy, but they were always in the right place at the right time.

We realized early on that we could feast off the pick-and-roll. The first time down, I set the pick, and he came off and raised up for a three pointer. I knew it was good when it left his hands, and the guy guarding him must have too because from that point on he started playing way more aggressive on defense.

Even with the guy hounding Dre, our team was still able to keep the game close. The score was tied as we entered the last minute of the game, and as Dre brought the ball up the court, I noticed him look my way just slightly.

I don't know how to explain it, but once we made eye contact, I knew without him having to say a word that he wanted me to cut toward the basket. At that very moment Dre dished what might be the best pass I've ever been on the receiving end for. Instead of throwing it to where I was, he threw it to where I was supposed to be, and thankfully I was there.

When it comes to dunking a basketball, I jump off of two feet instead of one, which means that I rarely get to catch a defender by surprise. That is unless I get a perfectly timed pass like the one Dre threw me. Him throwing it ahead of me instead of right to me meant that all I had to do was step into it without having to slow down my momentum to bring my feet together.

As soon as I caught the ball, I took flight. By the time the guy guarding me could look up, I was already looking down at the rim. Once I landed, all I could hear was the guys yelling and Dre saying, "Good work, Bama." It felt like home... except for the Bama thing of course, but whatever.

Another great part of the trip has been being able to chop it up with Mr. Dunbar. I've known him since freshman year, but after Capstone and this trip, he feels less like a teacher and more like an uncle. Given that, I stay true to my word and agree to give Harold's Chicken Shack and their mild sauce a shot.

As soon as we walk in, I do a quick glance over, and it gives me good wing spot vibes—like it's clean, but not too clean. The staff is cool, too, but not in that unnecessarily loud, I'm-just-doing-this-so-I-won't-get-fired kind of way.

They have a portrait of the founder, Mr. Harold Pierce, in the front. A framed article reads he was born in Midway, Alabama, and came to Chicago in 1943. He

worked as a chauffeur for seven years before starting

the first Harold's in 1950. I instantly make a mental note

that if the food actually does turn out to be good, I will

say it's because Harold's from the crib. Yes, I use crib to

claim people from Alabama too. No, I'm not ashamed.

Mr. Dunbar orders a six piece, fried hard, salt and

pepper, with mild sauce. I figure he knows the menu the

best, so I order the same thing. I gotta admit though, I'm

skeptical about the mild sauce. Mild isn't exactly a title

that excites me. Seems like a lukewarm word by

design, but whatever.

While we're waiting for our food, we make casual

small talk about the trip. The mood shifts when he

mentions graduation coming up though.

"I saw that you were named a finalist for the High

School Heisman the other day. Congratulations. That's a

wonderful accomplishment. I know that honor is

reserved for the top high school scholar athletes across the country."

"Thanks. I appreciate it."

"Have you thought any more about your next steps after graduation?"

"I still haven't made up my mind on where I want to go. I was waiting to see what might happen as far as basketball…but…nothing's really happening on that front."

"*Hmmm.* I can see that's bothering you. I won't force you, but I'm here if you want to talk."

"I guess it's just that basketball has always been a known for me. I don't know what I want to do career wise yet, but I've known since I was five that I'm a hooper. I know I'm more than that, but I've never been less than that. Basketball is even how I've made most of my friends, so I guess I just don't know what things would feel like without it."

"I can see how that would be tough to deal with. I have a question for you: What is your vision of success?"

"My vision of success?"

"Yes. When you look back on your life, what will you need to have accomplished in order to consider that your life was a success?"

"I never really thought of that…I guess I just want to be someone who was always there for my family and people in general and who made a positive impact."

"Okay. You didn't mention basketball. Why is that?"

"I guess it just didn't come to mind."

"Okay. The reason I asked is because I know you enjoy basketball and that it has played a big role in your life up to this point, but you have so much more life to live. I'm not saying that you're going to stop enjoying the game, but it won't always seem as important as it does now. That doesn't change what you're feeling at this moment. Your feelings are your feelings, and those are real. I'm just trying to give you some perspective. Do you remember the first girl you had a crush on?"

"Of course. My kindergarten teacher, Ms. Hill."

"Okay… That's not the answer I was expecting, but I'll work with it. How old were you?"

"I was five."

"Okay. Do you still have feelings for Ms. Hill now, or have the last thirteen years opened your eyes to other women, specifically those in your age group?"

"Well, I haven't seen her in a while, but I'm sure she's still fine. I get your point though."

"Okay. So what I'm trying to get you to see is that as you move through life, basketball will still bring to mind some great memories, life lessons, and hopefully lifelong friendships, but the importance of the game itself will diminish. That's regardless of whether you play in college or not. Do you understand?"

"Yes, sir."

Mr. Dunbar and I are definitely in the middle of a real moment, but these wings and this sauce though…may be the best combination I've ever tasted. I wish I would have ordered a ten piece, but my pride won't let me order more now because Mr. Dunbar would never let me hear the end of it.

"Have you thought about trying to walk on?"

"I have. I haven't talked to any coaches or anything about it yet though."

"Okay. There's nothing stopping you from trying to walk on at one of the schools that offers you an academic scholarship, if you decide to do that, but regardless of the outcome, I need you to leave this table knowing that basketball is only something you do. It's far from who you are."

"Yes, sir. Thank you."

"You're welcome. Are you familiar with Dikembe Mutombo?"

"Of course. I always stay up on the guys from Africa, even the OGs."

"Okay. Do you know where he went to college?"

"Yeah. Georgetown, right?"

"Yes, that's right. Did you know he attended on an academic scholarship?"

"Oh, wow. Really?"

"Yes, He was a very bright student growing up in the Congo and was awarded a scholarship by the U.S. federal government to study medicine. Once he made it to campus, John Thompson, the head basketball coach, kept hearing about a seven-foot- two student he had to meet. Dikembe eventually joined the team, and the rest is history. However, he never lost sight of his original aspiration. He eventually funded the opening of a hospital named after his late mother. The Biamba Marie Mutombo Hospital is located in his hometown, the capital city of Kinshasa, and it provides the highest level of patient care and research in the region. So yes he's an NBA Hall of Famer, but he's also much more than

that, and I see the same type of potential in you."

"Thanks, Mr. Dunbar. I appreciate that."

"It's true. As you consider colleges, I encourage

you to select a place that will both challenge and support

you to reach your full potential because you may even

surprise yourself with what you're capable of. With that

in mind, there's something I would like for you to

consider. Are you familiar with my alma mater, North

Carolina A&T?"

"Yeah. I know about A&T. It's in Greensboro,

right?"

"That's right. I asked because just last week I was

talking with one of my friends from undergrad who now

serves as the director of admissions for the university.

He shared that they're looking for candidates for their

Cheatham-White Scholars Program. The award is

named in honor of Henry P. Cheatham and George H.

White, two African-Americans who represented North

Carolina in the U.S. Congress in the early 1900s. It's for students who demonstrate high academic aptitude, leadership potential, and a strong commitment to service. I instantly thought of you when I learned of it. The award provides a fully funded four-year scholarship, as well as funds for summer enrichment, including the option to potentially study abroad. It's a competitive process, but if you're interested, I'm willing to serve as a recommender for you."

"I'm down. What would I need to do?"

"Well, talk to your parents first, and once they give the okay, then we can get started on the application."

"Will do. I really appreciate you, Mr. Dunbar. Seriously."

"Anytime. I'd love to have you be a fellow Aggie. My niece, Katrina, from my wife's side will actually be attending A&T next year. We always joke that she looks like my wife's twin. She's currently attending Whitney

Young over on the Westside, but she's planning to study mechanical engineering at A&T."

"Say less. I mean that's wassup."

North Carolina A&T? *Hmmm...*Sounds like a cool opportunity, and now that I think about it, their colors are yellow and blue.... Could be a sign.

Epilogue

Two Months Later

Capstone Day started off on a high with our class surprising Mr. Dunbar with a cake and a card that we all signed for his birthday. We all agreed that we had to do something special for him before the semester ended, and the cake and card were a no-brainer once we found out from one of our classmates that he has a May birthday.

The presentations for Capstone Day happened in the school auditorium, and parents and guests started arriving about an hour into the school day, so we knew we'd have to move quick to have time for the surprise. We figured Mr. Dunbar would head straight to the auditorium when he got to school that morning, so we made sure to all be in place and worked with the principal to have the cake already on stage.

As soon as Mr. Dunbar walked in and flipped on the lights, we started singing "Happy Birthday." He was so surprised that he was speechless for a few seconds, and it seemed like he even got a little choked up. Once he did start talking, he told us how much he appreciated us as a class and that we didn't have to do anything for him because our commitment this semester was already enough of a gift.

Once the program started, Mr. Dunbar welcomed all the guests in the audience and explained the motivation behind our Capstone project assignment. Then he told them they were in for a treat because our class was the most creative group of young people he'd ever had the opportunity to work with.

That comment drew a lot of positive feedback from our class backstage, topped off by one of my classmates yelling, "You're the real MVP, Mr. Dunbar," which made everyone in the auditorium burst into laughter.

Then it was showtime. Juice presented first, and he ended by bringing his grandma on his dad's side, Mrs. Augustus, on stage with him to do the Griddy dance he does whenever he scores a touchdown. We learned from his presentation that Mrs. Augustus is actually from New Orleans, where the dance originated from. Juice had music playing throughout his whole presentation, so people were already nodding their heads as Mrs. Augustus walked up to the stage. But when she took her jacket off to show an LSU jersey that read "Ms. Juice" on the back, the crowd went *wild*.

Up to that point no one outside of Juice's family had known he was going to LSU but me. He had told me the week before and asked me to keep it a secret because he was going to make an announcement at school. Even I didn't know he was going to reveal the news during his Capstone presentation though. From that point on, every other presentation just built on that energy.

When the time came for me to present, I couldn't help but laugh as I thought about how everything had come together. During our flight back from Chicago, I had mentioned to Mr. Dunbar that I was worried about not having settled on an idea for my presentation yet. He told me to relax and that the right idea would come to me eventually.

We landed in Birmingham on a Friday evening around six 'o clock. After eating dinner and catching up with Mom, Dad, and Ìfẹ́, I laid down because I knew I was on schedule for a volunteer reading coach session Saturday morning at the Pratt City Library. I always enjoy my reading coach sessions because I love working with the younger kids in the neighborhood, mostly because they're hilarious.

As a reading coach, I get paired up for thirty-minute sessions with second or third graders to offer some additional encouragement and assistance with their reading. The goal is to make reading fun, so the kids usually either bring a favorite book from home, or I let them pick one off the library shelves. I let the kids lead the way, and I only step in if they need help sounding out a word or if they have questions about what a word means. My main goal is to make sure the kids know I'm there to help if they need anything.

On this particular Saturday morning, it was such a beautiful day outside that I decided to walk to the library instead of driving. The library is only about a ten-minute walk from my house, and after dealing with Chicago's version of spring, I wanted to get as much sunlight as possible. Once I made it to the library, I spoke to the staff for a few minutes before taking a seat in the designated reading coach zone and waiting for any kids to arrive.

After about ten minutes passed, I noticed a little girl walking toward me with what turned out to be her grandmother. The first thing that caught my eye was the beads the girl wore in her hair. They reminded me of Ìfẹ́ when she was that age, and that made me smile. The next thing I noticed was the purple Parker High School class reunion t-shirt that her grandmother was wearing, and at that very moment I remembered that I was wearing a Ramsay basketball t-shirt. I smiled and introduced myself to both of them, and they introduced themselves as well.

Just as the grandmother was about to walk away to allow us to begin the session, she looked at me smiling and said," Alright now, Mr. Ramsay, don't you go recruiting my granddaughter. She's already said that she wants to go to Parker High like her Gigi."

I laughed and said, "Yes, ma'am," and then we got started.

The young lady told me that her name was Kaari, but that I could call her Ky. When I told her that she could call me Tunde, the confused look on her face reminded me that I had introduced myself as Lewis to her and her grandmother. For a split second I thought about running down my typical Ancestry.com report to

explain why Tunde would make sense as a nickname for

me, but I decided against it.

Clearly Ky wasn't bothered though because she

just laughed and said," Okay, Mr. Tunde."

Ky told me that she was seven years old and that

she was in the second grade at South Hampton, the

school right up the street from the library, then she

looked up at me and said, "You're really tall. Are you a

basketball player or something?"

I laughed and said, "Yeah, basketball is one thing

I do. What do you like to do though?"

She smiled and told me that she loved to dance,

but that she also liked soccer.

I smiled back and told her that I was sure she was

an amazing dancer and soccer player.

After we made some more small talk, which

ended in me committing to attend one of her upcoming

dance recitals, I asked Ky to tell me about the book she

had brought with her. As she laid it on the table in front

of us, she told me that it was one of her favorite books to

read whenever she was at her grandma's house.

I looked down at the book and instantly

recognized the title and author, *The Negro Speaks of

Rivers* by Langston Hughes. I was familiar with the poem

because we learned about it in school, even though it

had been a while since I'd read it. I'd never known there

was a picture book version though. The cover of the

book had a drawing of an older man and what I assumed

was his grandson out fishing by a river as the sun was

setting in the background. I know you're not supposed to

judge books by their covers, but I do, and this one

caught my attention.

Once we got started Ky did such an amazing job

reading the first few pages that I was more focused on

her than listening to the actual poem itself. I was paying

attention to the words, but since I was already familiar

with the poem, I wasn't expecting to come across

anything new. That is until she read one line that grabbed ahold of me in a way that I'd never experienced before.

I'm used to reading something in a book and thinking, *I've seen that before*, but when Ky read the line about the author's soul having grown deep like the rivers, my first thought was *I've felt that before*. I felt like those words summed up my whole experience of working on my Capstone project. I knew then that the poem was a must for my presentation, but what I didn't know was that I had forgotten to turn to the next page. That is until I felt Ky pat me on the arm and say, "Mr. Tunde, are you okay?"

I smiled and said, "Yes, Ky. I'm sorry," and she smiled back and kept reading.

We continued on until we made it all the way to the end of the book, and Ky did an amazing job. I told her how proud I was of her as I walked her back to her grandma, and I made sure to save the date for her next dance recital in my phone. I had the poem on my mind for the rest of that day though. Once I got home, I did some research on the poem, and I learned that Langston Hughes was actually my age when he wrote it. He was on a train ride to visit his father when he looked out the window and saw the Mississippi River. At that moment, he thought about what rivers had meant to our people and how "in a sense, our history was linked to the river."

So, as I prepared to start my Capstone presentation by reciting *The Negro Speaks of Rivers,* I had to smile as I thought of Ky and her grandmother. The poem was a perfect tone-setter for my presentation because Hughes doesn't only reference rivers in America, but he mentions the Congo and the Nile, too, so it was a great lead-in for me telling a story that spanned from North Birmingham to Nigeria.

In other news… I got the scholarship to A&T! Mr. and Mrs. Dunbar invited our family to dinner at their house to celebrate once we got the news. The dinner was great, but the highlight of the night was when I went into the kitchen to help Mrs. Dunbar grab something from the top shelf. She was in the kitchen Face Timing her niece Katrina who I can now confirm does look exactly like her, which is all the proof I needed that God is real. Anyway, Mrs. Dunbar introduced me and told Katrina that I'd be coming to A&T too. We didn't say much more than hi, but as I was walking out of the kitchen, I overheard Katrina say, "You didn't tell me he was taller than Uncle Aaron. He's cute."

Ìfẹ́ said I haven't stopped smiling since, and she's probably right.

As we were getting ready to leave, Mrs. Dunbar showed us where they had placed Mr. Dunbar's birthday card from our class on the mantel in their living room. She smiled as she told us that Mr. Dunbar and his daughters had read it every morning since we'd given it to him.

As everyone else was heading outside, Ìfẹ́ asked me to point out what I had written. After reading it, she looked at me smiling and said, "There may be hope for you after all, Lewis. What you lack in fashion, you make up for with being pretty good with words."

I laughed and said, "Whatever, Ìfẹ́," as she walked toward the front door. I was about to follow right behind her, but I paused for a moment before leaving to re-read what I had written in the card one more time…

Thank you for everything! I'm looking forward to seeing you at an A&T basketball game next year, and I'll definitely come back to visit whenever I'm in town. As the proverb says, "Odò kì í ṣàn kó gbàgbé ìsun"—*A river does not flow and forget its source." Happy Birthday, and Many Happy Returns.*